Alex + Kim,
Thought you
might like to try
some of these recipes
with Mom + Dad's help.
Love,
Aunt Barbara

The Teddy Bears' Picnic Cookbook

TEDDY BEARS' PICNIC COOKBOOK

by Abigail Darling
illustrated by Alexandra Day

Viking

VIKING
Published by the Penguin Group
Viking Penguin, a division of Penguin Books USA Inc.,
375 Hudson Street, New York, New York 10014. U.S.A.
Penguin Books Ltd, 27 Wrights Lane, London W8 5TZ, England
Penguin Books Australia Ltd, Ringwood, Victoria, Australia
Penguin Books Canada Ltd, 2801 John Street, Markham, Ontario, Canada L3R 1B4
Penguin Books (N.Z.) Ltd. 182–190 Wairau Road, Auckland 10, New Zealand

Penguin Books Ltd, Registered Offices: Harmondsworth, Middlesex, England

First published in 1991 by Viking Penguin, a division of Penguin Books USA Inc.

1   3   5   7   9   10   8   6   4   2

Text copyright © Abigail O'Hara, 1991
Illustrations copyright © Alexandra Day, 1991
Book Design by The Blue Lantern Studio
All rights reserved
Library of Congress Card Catalog Number: 90-55695
I S B N   0 - 6 7 0 - 8 2 9 4 7 - 1
Printed in Hong Kong
Set in ITC Bookman Light

INTRODUCTION

Picnics are a way for teddy bears and children to enjoy cooking, eating, and spending time out of doors. Because teddy bears have paws, not hands, the recipes in this book are simple and easy to make, but an adult is needed to help with sharp knives and hot stoves. Each picnic will serve four children or teddies.

With some planning, a picnic can be fun at any time of year. Where can you have a picnic? There are all the places you are used to thinking about, like parks and the beach. But how about your backyard or porch, or even indoors? Use your imagination!

Sometimes teddy bears don't have time to prepare a whole picnic, so they just have a simple meal like bread, cheese, and fruit, or they add something ready-made like cookies or little puddings. A picnic doesn't have to be fancy to be fun.

Tips to Help You Be a Good, Safe Chef

COOKING
——read the recipe all the way through before you begin, to make sure you understand it and that you have everything you need
——wear an apron, and wash your hands before you begin
——take out everything you will be using
——if any fruits or vegetables are called for, wash and dry them

SAFETY

—ask a grown-up to help when you need to use the oven or stove, or any sharp utensils

—when using a knife or peeler, cut away from your body

—always use pot holders when handling hot dishes or pots

—turn off the oven or stove as soon as you are done using it

—when cooking on top of the stove, point pot handles toward the center, so that they cannot be easily knocked off

CLEANUP

Be sure to leave the kitchen clean so that your parents will be glad to let you use the kitchen again. And always be sure not to leave anything behind at your picnic spot. Make it look as if you were never there, and if other people have left trash, pick that up, too. Teddy bears love and respect their world.

Packing

To go on a picnic, you will need something to put the food in. If you don't have a picnic basket, use a backpack, a tote bag, or the basket of your bicycle.

The recipes in this book give instructions for packing, but here are some more tips to help you pack food.

——salads or delicate fruit should be packed in plastic containers with lids

——liquids, such as soups or beverages, should be packed in a thermos

——sandwiches or bread can be wrapped in aluminum foil or plastic wrap. Fruits, vegetables, cookies, or crackers can be put in plastic bags.

When packing up your picnic food, be sure to put anything that could be crushed, like cookies or chips, on top.

Be sure to take along plates or bowls, eating utensils, and cups.

BREAKFAST PICNIC

It may seem that breakfast is not a picnic meal, but a morning picnic can be fun. The world is beautiful early in the day, and you will see different things from those you would see in the afternoon. Parks and other public places will be less crowded. Teddy bears like to go on morning picnics in the summertime, so they can enjoy the sunshine before it is too hot for their furry selves. This picnic is quick to prepare.

• MENU •

Scrambled Egg Sandwiches
Yogurt and Juice Shake-Up
Oranges

SCRAMBLED EGG SANDWICHES

After you have made these sandwiches once, try a little creativity. Add some minced vegetables, like tomatoes or green onions, to the eggs. Or place a slice of ham on top of the eggs and cheese.

EQUIPMENT
bowl, fork, measuring cup, frying pan, wooden spoon

TO PACK
aluminum foil

INGREDIENTS
2 tablespoons butter
6 eggs
¼ cup milk
1 cup grated cheese
4 English muffins
butter for buttering muffins

Break the eggs into the bowl, add milk, and mix well with fork. Over low heat, melt butter in frying pan. Tip the pan gently so butter coats bottom of pan, and pour in the egg/milk mixture. Stir the eggs gently with wooden spoon while they cook. When the eggs are no longer runny, sprinkle with the grated cheese and put a lid on the frying pan. Turn off heat.

Now toast and butter muffins. Put equal amounts of the egg/cheese mixture on four of the English muffin halves, then cover with the other four English muffins halves. Wrap each sandwich tightly in aluminum foil to keep it warm.

YOGURT AND JUICE SHAKE-UP

This drink will give you energy for the day ahead.

EQUIPMENT
large jar with lid, measuring cup

TO PACK
thermos with a 6-cup capacity

INGREDIENTS
3 cups fruit juice
1 eight ounce container of vanilla yogurt

Place the ingredients in the jar, and screw the lid on tightly.
Shake until the juice and yogurt are combined well. Pour in
thermos.

It may seem as though rainy days and picnics don't fit together very well. But teddy bears are optimists, which means they try to find joy in everything. They know that rain is important for plants and flowers, and from plants and flowers comes honey.

A wet afternoon is a fine time to read, play games, or draw pictures. Another good activity (and a favorite of always-hungry teddies!) is to plan, cook, and eat a meal. Spread a blanket on the floor, and enjoy this warming indoor picnic.

• MENU •

Vegetable Soup
Bread or crackers
Baked Apples
Milk

VEGETABLE SOUP

EQUIPMENT
large pot with lid, measuring cups and spoons, wooden spoon,
    ladle

INGREDIENTS
3 tablespoons olive oil
1 teaspoon Italian seasoning (a mixture of herbs like oregano
    and basil)
4 cups of water
2 beef bouillon cubes
1 small (8 ounce) can garbanzo or kidney beans
1 large can (15 ounce) tomato sauce
2 cups frozen vegetables (a 10-ounce package): you can use
    mixed vegetables, peas and carrots, or green beans
1 cup small pasta shells or macaroni, uncooked

　　Place all the ingredients in the pot. Mix with the wooden
spoon, put lid on the pot, and heat over low heat for 30 minutes.
Test the pasta to see if it is soft by eating one, then serve in
bowls using the ladle.

BAKED APPLES

EQUIPMENT
8 inch cake pan, apple corer, measuring cups and spoons

INGREDIENTS
4 apples, washed and cored (you may need adult help in coring
     the apples)
4 tablespoons brown sugar
1 teaspoon cinnamon
1 cup water
½ stick (¼ cup) butter

Preheat oven to 350 degrees

   Grease the pan by rubbing it with butter and place apples
in pan. Cut the rest of the butter into four pieces, and put
one piece inside each of the apples. Mix the brown sugar,
cinnamon, and water in bowl, and pour over the apples. Bake
for 30 minutes. Serve warm.

BACKYARD TEA PARTY

Teddies love all kinds of parties and celebrations, but they truly love tea parties. At a tea party, teddy bears can eat many sweets, including their favorite, honey. Lady bears wear their lacy white gloves and hats with flowers, and speak to one another of important things. Gentlemen bears often put on top hats, and try to behave well and not spill.

You can give a tea party for your friends, family, or teddies. Try to make everything as pretty as possible, with flowers and nice teacups and saucers (but remember to ask your parents' permission!). This party needs to be on a table. In a yard or on a porch or patio is perfect.

• MENU •

Tea with Milk and Honey
Little Sandwiches
Strawberries and Cookies

TEA WITH MILK AND HONEY

EQUIPMENT
teapot, measuring cups and spoons, kettle

INGREDIENTS
2 tea bags
½ cup milk
3 tablespoons honey

Fill the kettle with water, and put it on stove over high heat to boil. Place tea bags and honey in teapot. Now fill the teapot with boiling water, and let sit for five minutes (this is called "steeping" the tea). Add the milk and serve in teacups. Teddy bears might add more honey to their cups, and you can too, if you like.

LITTLE SANDWICHES

EQUIPMENT
long, serrated knife, cutting board, butter knife

INGREDIENTS
10 slices bread
smooth peanut butter
jam or honey (OPTIONAL)

Spread five slices of the bread with peanut butter, and jam or honey if you like. Top with other five slices of bread, so that you now have five sandwiches. Using the serrated knife and working on top of the cutting board, first trim the crusts off the sandwiches, then cut into the patterns pictured below.

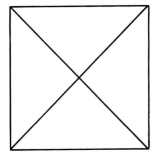 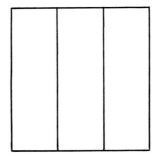 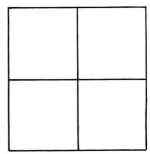

Serve on a large plate.

STRAWBERRIES AND COOKIES

This is a recipe that can be changed to suit your tastes and the season. If strawberries are not available, canned peaches would be a good substitute. Cookies that would be good choices are vanilla wafers, shortbread cookies, or lemon sandwich cookies.

EQUIPMENT
small knife, cutting board, colander

INGREDIENTS
1 basket strawberries
an assortment of cookies

Wash and drain the strawberries in colander. Working on the cutting board, cut the green top off each berry. Serve the berries in small bowls (clear glass ones look very pretty), and the cookies on small plates.

PICNIC á la FRANCE

Teddy bears and the people of France are a lot alike. They like to wear fashionable clothes, especially hats. Eating and preparing good food is something both teddies and French people enjoy a great deal. French food is famous all over the world because it is so delicious.

Teddies, who like to seem sophisticated, love French food. The little bears study fancy cookbooks, and try out new recipes. You can expand your culinary horizons with this simple French outdoor meal. Remember to take along your "chapeaux," and say "Bon appetit!"

• MENU •

Croissant Sandwiches
Crudités
Truffles au chocolat
(chocolate candies)
Grape Juice or Eau Minerale

CROISSANT SANDWICHES

Croissants are a delicious type of bread that are as French as the Eiffel Tower. They make lovely sandwiches.

EQUIPMENT
serrated knife, cutting board, butter knife

TO PACK
aluminum foil or sandwich bags

INGREDIENTS
4 croissants
8 slices of cheese
    AND/OR
4 slices of ham
mustard, butter, mayonnaise

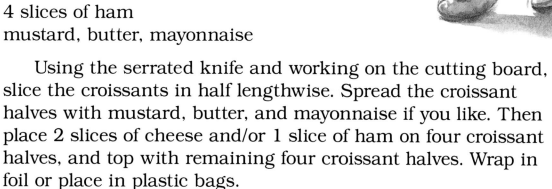

Using the serrated knife and working on the cutting board, slice the croissants in half lengthwise. Spread the croissant halves with mustard, butter, and mayonnaise if you like. Then place 2 slices of cheese and/or 1 slice of ham on four croissant halves, and top with remaining four croissant halves. Wrap in foil or place in plastic bags.

CRUDITÉS

Crudités (pronounced crew-ditt-AYS) is just a fancy French term for cut-up raw vegetables. The French believe it is a healthy, low-calorie way to fill up before meals. Teddy bears do not worry about their weight, but they do like vegetables.

Choose your favorite vegetables, cut them into bite-sized pieces, and pack in a plastic bag.

SUGGESTED VEGETABLES
carrots, celery, cherry tomatoes (these don't need to be cut),
    bell peppers, cauliflower, cucumber, Chinese peas, radishes

TRUFFLES AU CHOCOLAT

Truffles are named after a rare and delicious kind of mushroom. In France truffles are hunted by pigs who sniff the ground to find them. These truffles are made with chocolate.

EQUIPMENT
small saucepan, bowl that fits on top of saucepan, small plate,
    measuring cups and spoons, large plate, fork, teaspoon,
    butter knife

TO PACK
small plastic container with lid

INGREDIENTS
1 cup chocolate chips
½ stick (¼ cup) butter cut into small pieces
½ teaspoon vanilla
¼ cup cocoa, ¼ cup confectioner's powdered sugar,
    mixed together

Place chocolate chips, vanilla, and butter in bowl. Cover bowl with small plate. Half fill saucepan with water and heat until it boils. Turn off heat and place covered bowl over hot water. After 10 minutes remove bowl, and mix with fork. Refrigerate for 1 hour. Place cocoa/confectioner's sugar on large plate. Using a teaspoon, make balls of the cold chocolate about the size of large marbles. Roll in the sugar/cocoa mixture, and place in container. Keep refrigerated until you are ready to leave for your picnic.

WARM WINTERY PICNIC

Teddy bears are well-dressed for winter, which they enjoy very much. Often they will be caught frolicking in the snow, and when there are wet footprints on the floor, sometimes teddies are to blame.

Picnics in winter can be great fun. Dress warmly, and bring warm food. Find a dry place to sit, or bring something to sit on. If you see some teddy bears nearby, take them for a sleigh ride or help them build a snowman.

• MENU •

Stuffed Baked Potatoes
Honey Hot Chocolate
Graham Crackers

STUFFED BAKED POTATOES

EQUIPMENT
serrated knife, bowl, fork, measuring cup, spoon, grater

TO PACK
aluminum foil

INGREDIENTS
4 small potatoes
1 loosely packed cup
    of grated cheese
4 tablespoons (½ stick)
    of butter at room
    temperature

Preheat oven to 450 degrees

Bake potatoes for 45 minutes, or until fork goes in easily. Take potatoes out of oven and cut in half with serrated knife, but do not cut all the way through. Using spoon, scoop out the insides of the potatoes into a bowl and add butter and cheese. Mix well with fork and place the potato back into the potato skins. Press the potatoes back together, and wrap tightly in aluminum foil to keep them warm.

HONEY HOT CHOCOLATE

EQUIPMENT
medium-sized pan, wooden spoon,
    measuring cups and spoons,
    fork, rubber spatula

TO PACK
thermos with a 4-cup, or large, capacity

INGREDIENTS
4 tablespoons cocoa
4 tablespoons honey
4 cups milk

Put cocoa in a cup with a little of the milk (about 3 tablespoons) and mix well with fork until you have a smooth paste. Using the rubber spatula, scrape the cocoa mixture into the pan, then add the remaining milk and the honey. Heat over low heat, stirring occasionally for 5 minutes. Pour cocoa into thermos. Be sure to take along plastic or metal mugs. Warm cups feel nice on cold hands or paws.

Teddy bears, like children, celebrate their birthdays with their families. But that is no reason not to have an extra birthday party for a friend or family member. Toys and pets have birthdays, too, and would enjoy a party. A birthday party needs a cake, which is a big job for a teddy bear. Ask your parents to get you one from the market or bakery. Maybe you and your parents could make a cake together, the night before the party. Use pretty paper plates and napkins, and bring along party hats to make your birthday picnic festive.

• MENU •

Vegetable and Cheese Pitas
Fruit Fizz Punch
Pretzels and Potato Chips
Cake

VEGETABLE AND CHEESE PITAS

EQUIPMENT
bowl, fork, knife, cutting board, grater

TO PACK
aluminum foil

INGREDIENTS
1½ cups grated cheese
1 carrot, grated
1 stalk celery, chopped
1 tomato, chopped
4 tablespoons Italian salad dressing
4 pita breads

　　Place all the ingredients except the pita bread in a bowl, and mix lightly with fork. Cut the pita breads in half, and in each half spoon in some cheese/vegetable mixture. Wrap each pair of halves in aluminum foil.

FRUIT FIZZ PUNCH

EQUIPMENT
no cooking utensils are needed for this recipe

TO PACK
a large, resealable plastic bag

INGREDIENTS
1 liter soda
1 quart fruit juice
ice

Take along on your picnic the soda and juice, and some ice cubes in the plastic bag. Put some ice in each picnicker's glass, and then pour in equal amounts of juice and soda. Some good juice and soda mixtures would be:
——cranberry juice cocktail and club soda
——apple juice and ginger ale
——orange juice and lemon-lime soda

MORE PICNIC FOODS

SANDWICHES

Sandwiches, of course, are the most popular and easy picnic food.
Here are lists of suggestions for different fillings and breads.

Fillings	*Breads*
Peanut butter and jam, jelly, or raisins	White, wheat, sourdough, or rye bread
Cheese	Raisin bread
Bologna, or other sandwich meats	Pita bread
Meat loaf	Bagels
Tuna, egg, or chicken salad	English muffins
Grated cheese, mixed with cut-up vegetables and salad dressing	Rolls
	Croissants

MAIN DISHES OTHER THAN SANDWICHES

Soup in a thermos
English muffin pizza

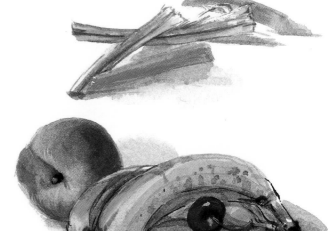

SIDE DISHES

Carrot and celery sticks
Green salad
Macaroni or potato salad
Small bags of chips or pretzels

DESSERTS

Cookies
Doughnuts
Small candy bars
Trail mix
Fresh fruit
Dried fruit (like raisins, apricots, and apples)